Laura C. (Laura Carter) Holloway

Adelaide Neilson

A Souvenir

Laura C. (Laura Carter) Holloway

Adelaide Neilson
A Souvenir

ISBN/EAN: 9783337002756

Printed in Europe, USA, Canada, Australia, Japan

Cover: Foto ©Andreas Hilbeck / pixelio.de

More available books at **www.hansebooks.com**

ADELAIDE NEILSON

A SOUVENIR

BY

LAURA C. HOLLOWAY

ILLUSTRATED

FUNK & WAGNALLS:

NEW YORK,   1885.   LONDON,

10 AND 12 DEY STREET.   44 FLEET STREET.

LIST OF ILLUSTRATIONS.

Adelaide Neilson

SOUVENIR

ADELAIDE NEILSON.

" A thing of beauty is a joy forever."

"SHE wur a bonny lass, she wur, and niver quite like other lasses," said an old acquaintance who knew Adelaide Neilson in her early years in Yorkshire.

To picture her aright: to describe in what respects she differed from, and in what she was allied to her kind: to show the extent and the limit of hereditary and extraneous influences; and to reveal the degree to which she possessed the power of *recuperation*, which to us seems the best definition of genius, is the labor of love attempted.

Since we cannot account for certain exceptional talents that she possessed, except under the law of spontaneity, so likewise we must introduce the highest law of life—the spiritual, —to interpret some of the most beautiful manifestations of her genius. And we cannot make any judgment of it that does not include all the contradictions of her nature. She was a many-sided personality ; one difficult of analysis. Yet the chiefest difficulty lies not so much in realizing this as in interpreting conclusions to the world which knew her wholly through her characterization of imaginary beings. Stripped of the romance of the stage and the glamour thrown over one who reaches such dramatic eminence, it is pleasing to find her a very lovable and loving woman, one whose powers of fascination charmed and delighted all who came within her sphere. That she was not all she might have been endears her the more to generous minds, since we know that hers was an uncommonly hard lot in some vital particulars, and that she made her way through difficulties and under shadows which sometimes engulfed her, causing her to lose her way and sorely bruising herself, but never embittering her nature or shadowing the light that was within her and that shone forth brightest when the darkness without appeared akin to despair.

The woman who to the public seemed

> " A lovely apparition sent
> To be a moment's ornament,"

was one by nature sweet and reverent; strong and earnest of soul; loving, and forgiving.

Said one who loved her well, " When we know all that she forgave, then we shall know the measure of her great heart."

The personality of Miss Neilson was so charming ; the spell of her fascination was so enthraling, that it was not a matter of surprise that all sorts of extravagant stories regarding her antecedents and early surroundings were currently reported and received. It seemed the only natural solution of her beauty and great talents to believe that she was the offspring of a titled family, the child of truly great parents. Any theory at variance with preconceived personal notions regarding her antecedents was unsatisfactory; so that people came to think that she was none other than a "Maid of Saragossa;" a child of a race, of whose best physical type she seemed so glorious a representative.

> " Her eyes were stars of twilight fair,
> Like twilight, too, her dusky hair;
> A dancing shape, an image gay,
> To haunt, to startle, and waylay.
>
> . . . .
>
> And yet a spirit still, and bright,
> With something of an angel's light."

But Adelaide Neilson, with her southern face and ardent temperament, her sensuous beauty and tender grace, was not of the race or degree that was accredited to her, and in correcting this misjudgment it is well to correct also the false assumption that her beauty of person comprised her principal claim to admiration. Such a conclusion is both flippant and superficial. Her charm was spiritual, and it vivified her mind to that degree that the personality expressed it in outward signs and forms. Conventional standards of beauty were set aside in her case; it was the inexpressible quality that individualized her loveliness, and this quality is of the spirit. Miss Neilson, it will be remembered, was never a subject of ordinary admiration, she was really, sincerely loved. There was a something pervading her presence that created a glow in even cold hearts, and she was never seen with indifference. We have said that public opinion voted Miss Neilson a Spaniard, and her admirers strengthened the belief that she was a Southerner. Miss Neilson herself lent color to this conviction by her silence on the subject.

After her death the most fulsome of her biographers made her birthplace Saragossa, and her surroundings in childhood such as would seem most fitting to one of her temperament. And there lies before us a narrative, stating that her parents "educated her in the best schools of Italy and France, and prepared her for her brilliant career by every advantage

that wealth and opportunity could supply." Had such been the case Adelaide Neilson would never have possessed the interest to us that she does, or had the irresistible charm that made her so beloved. Social helps and hindrances counted for little in her case, for they were minor factors in it. In studying her life, one is strangely impelled to look beyond ordinary motives and circumstances; to form conclusions not reached by those who attribute organization to surroundings and great gifts to forces well understood.

" Who was she? and What was her heritage?" are questions asked by every one who saw her and felt the magnetic power she exerted.

Her history is in a sense an epitome of human existence, inasmuch as her nature was so full and rich that it touched in its varied and manifold phases all life's correspondencies. Its very inconsistencies made it richer.

The essential facts of her career are easy to relate, even if certain desirable details are lacking. The parentage of Adelaide Neilson on the father's side is doubtful. Of her mother much is known, though not of that mother's early life. For reasons of her own, Mrs. Bland has been reticent concerning this period, and the circumstances of her daughter's birth she has jealously guarded, probably because of the pain of exposure to the latter. Miss Neilson, in speaking of this fact concerning herself, to one or two intimate friends of later years, expressed deepest regret for it, yet never was heard to reflect by tone or word upon her mother for her misfortune. That she sorely grieved over it all her life her mother knew, and the indefinable shadow that was often upon her face, was reflected there by this living sorrow. This expression was often noted, but was not understood until the mother told the story of her daughter's discovery of the facts of her birth and the effect it had upon her.

The first authentic knowledge we have of Miss Neilson dates back to the close of her second year. At that time she was living at Skipton-in-Craven, England, with her mother, who was Miss Browne, and who was, previous to her daughter's birth, and for some months subsequent to it, an actress. Of Miss Browne's histrionic ability no account has come to us. She traveled with a stock company over what was known as the Northern Circuit, at a time when railroads and telegraphs were not, and the public to whose pleasure she catered did not interest itself, as now, in actors when off the stage. The young woman doubtless had her

triumphs and enjoyed the reward of her efforts
in the profession she followed. Miss Browne's
father was an English engraver, and is repre-
sented by his daughter as having been a work-
man proud of his art. Both her father and her
mother were Yorkshire people. She became
enamored of the stage and left her home while
quite young to seek her fortune upon it, and
was a girl in her teens when Adelaide was born.
Her marriage to Mr. Bland took place subsequently. The father of Adelaide Neilson was
an actor who was attached to a company in
Leeds when he first met Miss Browne. It is
conjectured that Adelaide was born there, but
Mrs. Bland, when asked regarding this point,
sternly refused to divulge the place or circumstance of her birth. She, however, was
born in Yorkshire, and at or near Leeds. Mrs.
Bland is authority for the statement that Adelaide's father was a Spaniard and that the personal beauty of her daughter was her inherit-
ance from the father whom she never knew.

Mr. Bland, whose occupation was that of a
painter and paper-hanger, was a native of the
neighborhood of Burnsall in Upper Wharfdale,
where he has a brother now living. The home of
the Blands immediately succeeding their union
was at Skipton-in-Craven. A relative of his
family gives the information that they lived in

that village two years, from 1848 to 1850, and
that when they left there, " Lizzie Ann," which
was the only name of our heroine until she
bought and paid for the one which, with one or
two modifications, she afterwards came to be
known by to the world, was four years old.
In her fifth year she went with her parents to
Guiseley, where the family established themselves in a part of the village known as Green
Bottom, a locality entirely changed of late
years by the railroad which now runs through
that part of the town. Their advent into Guiseley seems not to have created any uncommon
interest among the villagers, who do not appear
to have concerned themselves regarding the
past history of the couple. They settled down
to their humble style of living, and Mrs. Bland
in addition to her household cares added to the
family income by going out by the day as a
seamstress. She was evidently a woman of far
more ability and energy of character than her
husband, and her married life was full of toil
and care. Her children came rapidly until
twelve were born, and still she worked with her
needle to add to the comforts of life for her
family.

. . . .

No region of England is richer in historic interest than Yorkshire. No section rivals it in

natural beauty. The antiquarian loves it and finds in its ancient chapels, its remains of Druid's altars; its mountains, fortifications and Roman roadways; its quaint stone houses, successors to the castles and abbeys that once reared their stately turrets, a field of unfailing wealth. No locality has produced more or better local chroniclers than favored Yorkshire. Naturally, it has many attractions, and is picturesquely beautiful even now, when almost every hamlet is defiled with factory smoke, and the dun-covered moors are traversed by railroads. Over the moorlands sounded the curfew from church belfries coeval with Canterbury and York; and through its grey fields have traveled some of England's most renowned men and women—Yorkshire children born and bred. John Wickliffe, the "morning star of the Reformation," was born in the North Riding of Yorkshire, and Whitefield and Wesley came to teach its sturdy sons the way of salvation through Methodism. Here, too, in a moorland village, now famous for all time, lived and died the Bronte sisters, who have given to the Yorkshire of this century a greater interest than its rich abbeys or its antiquity made for it in the past.

The manufacturers long ago invaded the Yorkshire region and built upon its hillsides

and watercourses their huge, ugly structures;
while the people of that section have been
brought into closer relations with the outside
world, by reason of the railroads which now
traverse the entire district. All the inland
villages have felt the impetus of commerce,
and the distances between them have been almost annihilated since the days of stage
coaches. Guiseley, like Haworth, has grown
considerably of late years, and in fact is now
too much of a place to be called a village. It
has not only a busy railroad station, but a town-
hall of considerable pretentions, and schools
and churches, where in Adelaide Neilson's
childhood it had only a school and a church.
The old style of living has changed much since
the days when hand-loom weaving was prose-
cuted at the fireside of the good, honest work-
ing people—a sturdy, independent race, and has
been slowly but surely supplanted by machin-
ery, and the daily incarceration in gloomy fac-
tories against which they could not compete.
To glance into any one of the houses of the
olden time was to see the loom, like a four-post
bedstead, all but filling up the room in which
the weavers worked, while stretched across the
ceiling the oatcake was strung up in long
rows, and the bacon flitch hung from the great
hooks in the beams. Now the provisions for

the household are all procured from some neighboring shop, with a running account to be "squeezed off," if possible, at the end of the week.

Guiseley people long ago put off the habits of their forefathers, and since it has grown to be a manufacturing town they have taken on the ways of other places. Hardly would they or their village be recognized by one who knew them thirty years ago. But even modernized as it is by its increase of wealth and population, no more discordant surroundings could have been found, apparently, for the development of a nature such as Adelaide Neilson possessed; on the other hand, perhaps, no better condition for the full display of pre-natal influences could have been devised. At least it is true, that in the case of no one have such influences been more potent and self-evident than in hers. The little girl who shared in the play of the children of Green Bottom, or did her appointed tasks as a "filler" in the factory near by, grew in delicate beauty and greater promise day by day beside those who realized her unlikeness to themselves, yet could not define it. She was a loving, winsome child, generous and unselfish in her home, and helpful to her mother in the care of the younger children. If any one understood her nature in those days it was her mother, but she does not appear to have fully comprehended her daughter. She, however, knew her better than anyone else, and noted with secret pleasure the fondness for learning that the child exhibited, and the bent of her mind in the direction of dramatic study. Mrs. Bland knew that her daughter's tastes were directly inherited from both her father and herself, and yet she seemed never to fully comprehend the inevitable consequences of fostering her natural likings. It was a motherly expression of her pride in her beautiful daughter that led her to dress her better than she did her other children and to clothe her in daintier raiment than her neighbors approved. And when she was chided for it she would defend herself by saying that she bought the clothing with her own earnings, and made it with her own hands. Her course in overdressing the child brought no harm to one who could not be spoiled by dress, as it was not her chief thought. She had an unconquerable desire to learn, and so long as she could go to school she was absorbed in her studies, and in her crude but strong interpretations of character parts. Whatever she read she made her own, and individualized it in delivery, to the delight of her fellow students.

Among the possessions of Mrs. Bland which

were associated with her history previous to
her marriage, were a number of plays, some
of them Shakespeare's, which were early in
the hands of her daughter. These were read
and re-read, until when she was eight years old
she could not only repeat long extracts from
them but intelligently act them. She would
often interrupt her mother to tell her how
passages should be recited, and would continue to read and re-read them until she satis-
fied her own ideal. She would lie in bed at night
reading and memorizing until the light would
be forcibly put out by her mother, and when-
ever she could not be found in the daytime the
latter would seek her in a room where in a
bureau drawer were kept the yellow-covered
plays that she did not permit others to handle.
There the young girl would be discovered, either
on the floor bent over the coveted book, or
walking the room conning some part that she
wished to make her own. Before she was
twelve years old she knew every play that
she had ever read, and could recite with entire correctness the tragedies of Shakespeare
which grown-up people find it difficult to learn.
She was deft with her needle, and improvised
costumes for her dolls with singular aptitude;
she, however, did not care for them as make-
believe babies, but as a sympathetic audience

before whom she could act and declaim. So
long as she was in the mood for mimic performances they were companionable, but when
she tired of playing the tragic queen, and
threw off the additional drapery, generally her
mother's apron, that had served as a train to
her short frock, she left the dolls to silence and
neglect until the mood returned. Always her
impersonations were tragic; when she was four
years old she was inventing and acting characters, and at five she had realized her con-
ception of a ghost. In great excitement she
hastened to her mother and tried to have her
see her interpret it, but the latter refused
and compelled her to desist from the attempt.
Her habit of memorizing, which was perfectly
natural and easy, made her a favorite pupil at
school, where her talent was often called into
requisition on anniversary occasions, or when
company was to be entertained. She was
studious, but it was clearly evident to her
teacher that her taste was decidedly literary,
and her bent was unmistakably dramatic.
Unfortunately she could not give as much
time to her favorite pursuits as she wished;
it would have delighted her to do nothing else,
but she was the eldest girl in a family where
daily labor had to be performed, and she did
not shirk her portion of it. She helped her

mother with the household work, and went out with her step-father to assist him in his business of paper hanging. Not a few rooms in Guiseley houses were papered by Mr. Bland with her help, and families are known there now who will not remove the paper that is associated with her, though it is faded and long out of fashion.

But no amount of work could quench her thirst for reading, and it is related by a shop-keeper of Guiseley that she would come to his store to get family supplies, and forget everything else in her interest in reading the signs and announcements in the place. When good-naturedly chided for not hastening home she would smilingly hurry away to her waiting mother, and repeat the same thing on every occasion. There was at this time, and for several years later, no outward sign of distaste for her surroundings, and perhaps no inner thought of rebellion against the fate that was hers. She was young, and was as happy as children are who are as affectionate and docile as was this little Yorkshire girl. The story of her childhood has been painted in cheerless colors by those to whom it doubtless appeared depressingly so, as compared with the era of opulence and fame that came to her. The chill of contrast is always severely

felt by those who judge exclusively by ex-
ternals.

Her rare possession was an imagination, rich
and fervid, and this was a compensation for
many of the trials she endured, absorbing her
so completely as to make her oftentimes obliv-
ious of disagreeable circumstances that would
have grated harshly upon her nerves. To an
unimaginative person hers doubtless seems
a bitter lot; but in her this faculty was so
highly developed that she lived a life of her
own, and reveled in scenes unreal and un-
dreamed of by others. It may appear absurd
to say that the very circumstances of her life
served as an impelling force in awakening the
intellectual tendencies of her nature. But,
driven back upon herself, the child found hap.
piness in her own way, and this was in study.

She never had the opportunity, as a child, of
seeing a first-class performance, but the traveling shows that came to Guiseley and the
neighboring village of Gibbs had frequent pa-
trons in Mrs. Bland and her daughter; and the
latter went home from each one fired with
new zeal and determination to be an actress.
Few persons ever gave more unmistakable evidence of inherited taste than did this young girl
for the stage. Her mother was secretly pleased
with the predilection her daughter manifested,

and did nothing to oppose her inclinations, if she did nothing to foster and develop her natural ability.

In her childhood there was no national school at Guiseley, and the little Lizzie attended the parochial school presided over by Mr. Frizell, who still resides there. Mr. Frizell perfectly remembers her as a quiet, attentive and studious child; one possessed of a wonderful memory and extraordinary talent for reciting. At the Primitive Methodist Church, where she was for years a regular attendant, she was especially remarkable for her quiet ways and gentle manners. Middle-aged women in Guiseley, who were her classmates in both schools there, recall her as the most studious among them, and always ready to read or recite, without the hesitation that they felt in appearing before strangers. An old lady, whose daughter was at school with her and worked beside her in the factory the short time that she was there, indignantly denied the report brought back to Guiseley, that a neighbor had seen Lizzie Ann play in Leeds.

"Lizzie a player!" she exclaimed; "Never. She wur naught but a book-learner." And it took some time to convince her that such was the case, and that her mother, Mrs. Bland, had been there and seen her for herself.

The necessity that compelled the future actress to go to work in the factory was not so
great but that it might have been averted; but
no one seems to have felt that she would be
different from others about her, and if any one
thought of her future it was not with the least
intuition of her great ability. She went to do
drudgery in a place utterly discordant to her;
and the change from school to factory cost her
untold anguish.

If at this turning-point in her career some
wise and beneficent friend had interfered in
her behalf and had her continue at her educa-
tion, how different might have been her life!
But no one came, and she dutifully earned the
pittance that was absorbed in the family, and
her mother saw the sacrifice, and seemed not
to realize it. No one recognized her genius
or spoke in its behalf. With her beautiful face,
gracious manners and soft, low voice, she was
utterly out of place in a factory; and it would
seem that her mother should have made an
effort at resistance to such an alternative.

We need not look further to find the key to
the causes that led the young girl to fly from
her home and all that knew her; nor should we
add one more unjust thought to any that may be
harbored against her for taking her fate into her
own hands. It was not that she did not love her

kindred and friends: she had the tenacious affection of a loving child for all about her, and what she suffered in leaving all behind her to make her way to distant Leeds and still more distant London, only she knew, and she could never refer to it without manifesting poignant sorrow.

The testimony of all those who knew her in her youth, unbroken and unimpeachable, is, that she was a docile, gentle and obliging child ; an industrious and unselfish girl, ready to do any work that came to hand, and despite her intellectual pre-eminence, which old and young alike acknowledged, never spoiled. Not even was she made vain by the fact that she was beautiful, though she knew that hers was a comely face to look upon. Almost any nature of like tenderness and innate refinement would have been destroyed by such antagonistic treatment as hers received, and it is saying the last conclusive words of evidence in her behalf, that she was never disloyal, never bitter against those who, by their blindness, made her life so hard.

One groans in bitterness over the blighting frost that settled so early in life upon the loving, trustful heart, and wonders that the brave spirit held its course.

Mr. Shuttleworth, a present resident of Guiseley, who lived there when the Blands removed to the village, remembers "Lizzie," as he still styles her, from her childhood. At twelve years of age she was a most ravenous reader. Meet her when he would she was holding some book or paper to her eyes, and so intent was she upon her reading that she often stumbled against people in the lanes, or would bang against some object that came in her way. He relates this incident illustrative of her strong dramatic instinct, which occurred when she was fourteen years old: Once she took a family, where she was visiting, by surprise, by giving a specimen of her dramatic ability. She had been reading aloud something of a tragic character in a book, and then she said, "If I were an actress, this is the way in which I should perform the scene I have just read you," and then she at once went through a marvelous piece of impersonation, which she ended by throwing herself upon a sofa and going off in a swoon—so naturally done that the household were thrown into the greatest alarm, believing it all to be real. She, however, soon set their fears at rest by springing from the sofa with a merry peal of laughter. The good folks did not encourage her to try the experiment again.

It was about this time that the young girl discovered the fact her mother had never

thought proper to tell her. The secret of her birth was unsuspected by others, it would appear, and became known to her by accident, on a day when she was searching a chest of drawers, one of which her mother kept locked and to which she carried the key. This day she had gone off for a day's sewing and had forgotten to take the key with her, and her daughter finding it, opened the drawer and looked through it. Her curiosity to know its contents may have induced her to disobey her parent, but it is as likely that she was in search of other plays, and hoped to find that some were concealed from her there. At all events she found a package of letters, and, delighted to have something to read, took them and examined their contents. One or more of them alluded to "the child" and others were of a nature to make the reader aware that she was connected with the mystery which she found in them. No sooner had her mother returned than she told her of her discovery and demanded an explanation. Confronted by the excited child, and fearing, most likely, to have a scene if she refused to tell her the truth, her mother took her where they could be alone and told her of her parentage. The fact that she was not the daughter of Mr. Bland, nor the sister of the children in her home, had a curi-

ous effect upon her. She said nothing to her
mother then or afterward regarding the revelation, but restlessness grew upon her and
her mother's influence was weakened. There
had never been very tender relations between
them, and after her sad discovery the girl did
not care to be at home. She went as nurse girl
to the family of Mr. John Padgett, at the Hawk-
hill House; sleeping at home nights and spend-
ing the days in the Padgett nursery, where she
was dearly loved by the little inmates. Her
employers have invariably spoken of her in
highest terms, and since her death they have
obligingly answered all inquiries concerning
her.

She was gradually weaned from the home
circle by the life she led, and when she finally
reached the determination to leave Guiseley
and seek employment elsewhere, the only person she told of her intention was the lady for
whom she worked, Mrs. Padgett. There have
been painful explanations made of her final
decision to leave home, which are put forward
as an extenuation of her conduct in not appris-
ing her mother of her intentions; but they are
not authentic, and are not essential to a full
understanding of the case by all who ever knew
the woman herself, or have had knowledge
of her character. She went to Mrs. Padgett's

house daily for two years, and was in her seventeenth year when she left her service. It has been said that she was younger by three years, but this is most likely the correct age. She was daily realizing the depressing influences that her distasteful life were having upon her, and yet she saw no remedy for it. Her personal charms were so noticeable that the young people joked her often about her admirers, but received in reply little encouragement to repeat their banter. On several occasions she said to her employer, in referring to these conversations, that she intended to be *something;* that she would not live in Guiseley all her life. Just what circumstance occurred that made her announce one day that she should give up her position and leave it that night, is not known. She was hardly believed to be in earnest, for, despite the unsatisfactory condition of things, she loved the home circle and clung to her mother as the nearest of all human beings to her. She communicated her intention of going to Mrs. Padgett, and that lady tried to dissuade her; finding, however, that persuasion would not avail, she paid her what was due for her services and saw her depart at nightfall to return no more.

"The unhappy girl cried bitterly," said Mrs. Padgett, in relating the incident years after, "and said she could not stay at home any longer; that she should go away and live; but I did not suppose she would leave that very night, alone and unprovided with sufficient clothing to make a journey." That night she went away, but was not missing until the next evening. Her mother, supposing her to be at her employment, felt no uneasiness until she failed to appear the second night, and when she learned that she was gone it was too late to overtake her, even had they known where to look for her.

Leaving Mrs. Padgett, the young girl walked to Apperly Bridge, where she took the train for Leeds, and on reaching there went to the house of an aunt who resided there. This aunt was an elderly woman, and was fond of her pretty niece who was so dutiful a child, and—what was of more importance in her eyes—was so faithful an attendant at Sunday-school. She seems not to have tried to exert any influence over her young relative, if she knew of her intention of going to Leeds, and the next day Lizzie left her and proceeded to London, which city she reached late in the day in a friendless condition.

After walking the streets, not knowing what to do, she sat down exhausted in Hyde Park late in the afternoon, and slept that night under the protecting shelter of the trees. Early in the morning she met a policeman to whom she told her condition and asked him to help her to get work. He took her to his own home, where she was kindly received by his wife, who was as completely convinced of the truth of her story as was her husband. The homeless, nameless girl made herself useful in the family and soon endeared herself to them by her fondness for their children and her sweet, obliging ways. Later on she sought a place where she could earn something, and obtained work as a seamstress. While sewing for small wages she went to the theatre on several occasions, and one day made her way to a manager and asked him for employment. Her beautiful face and pleasing manners helped her in securing a start, and in the humble place of ballet-girl, which was offered her, she earned money enough to buy needful and suitable clothing. Thus, in a short time after she had reached London, she had entered upon the career she had so ardently desired to follow, and had brought to it an intense and healthful ambition to excel in it.

Her superiority over the other ballet-girls was made manifest at once, and the stage-manager became so interested in her that he advanced her to a better place.

Her Yorkshire accent, which had convinced

the policeman whose aid she asked, that she
was from the country, was still too pronounced
to admit of her overcoming it without study,
and she was offered the opportunity to educate
herself by this manager, who was not only im-
pressed that she had high histrionic abilities,
but was also personally fascinated by her.
To his genuine interest she owed her start on
the career she made for herself. He helped
her at the turning point of her life and made
it possible for her to reach the dramatic rank
she subsequently acquired.

Acting on his advice, and with the pecuniary
aid offered her by him, she studied for two
years, making herself proficient in her line of
work and the cultivated woman she came to be.
She told Mr. Padgett, during her first visit to
Guiseley—in recounting to him her history subsequent to the time of her leaving there—that
during the years she was at school she devoted
eighteen out of the twenty-four to her studies,
and mastered seven languages.

Her first appearance was in 1865, as *Juliet*, at
Margate Theatre, then under the management
of the Messrs. Thorne. She made a success.
and a few weeks later she appeared at the Royalty Theatre in the same character, and at-
tracted the attention of the press and the public. Later on, she drew all London to Drury

Lane, to see her interpretation of *Amy Robsart*, and *Pauline.*

Subsequently, she played in the provinces and was everywhere received with delight. Her salary was rapidly increased, until she commanded in London £400 a week.

When the young girl left Guiseley she called herself Lizzie Bland, but as soon as she began her theatrical career she took the name of Lilian Adelaide Lessont, which she afterwards changed to Neilson, and legally owned. She was so poor when she began as not to have even a name of her own!

Six years from the time she left home, during which period she had never communicated with her family, or divulged her whereabouts, she made her first professional visit to Leeds. In that interval Mr. Bland had died, and Mrs. Bland and the surviving children were still living in the humblest circumstances in quiet Guiseley. Mrs. Bland had read in the newspapers that an actress of great beauty and celebrity was coming to Leeds to play, and having an intuitive idea that the lovely woman was her daughter, she went to the city to satisfy herself. She learned that the actress was stopping at the White Horse Hotel, Boar Lane, and going there and stating her errand, was admitted to the rooms of her daughter. The latter instantly recognized her and welcomed her affectionately, and when they parted, she to return to Guiseley and her daughter to London, she carried with her substantial proof of her child's interest in her. In a few months Miss Neilson returned to Leeds, and true to her promise, made a visit to her mother.

This visit was a hurried one, and was taken by Miss Neilson mainly for the purpose of placing her mother above want. She invested £3,000, the interest of which she settled upon her mother and left her in comfort.

On the occasion of her second visit, made in 1869, two years later, "her appearance at church," said Mr. Shuttleworth, who was the organist at that time, created such a *furore* that she was alarmed and refused afterward to appear on the street. Her resplendent beauty, and the superb apparel she wore, quite turned the heads of the quiet villagers, who climbed over pews and fought for an opportunity to see her. The contrast must have been striking between the young girl who had played in the streets and worked in the factory at Green Bottom, and the woman who was in the zenith of her fame and beauty. She was rich, and her jewels, the gifts of royalty and nobility, were valued at £10,000. The earrings that she wore were composed of two costly diamond *soli-*

taires, presents from the Russian and Austrian Ambassadors, and her ordinary dress was rich and beautiful. She was the same unaffectedly kind person she had ever been and her old friends were made happy in her coming among them. These visits to Guiseley were not happy ones to herself, however; they recalled too vividly the sufferings she had endured and the mistake she felt she had made in the manner of her departure from the village. A friend who knew her well in those days, states that she was keenly sensitive on this point and could never allude to her early life without expressing regret at her course—a course which this friend in common with others, thought entirely defensible in view of all the circumstances.

This same friend is authority also for this statement: that the happiest days of Miss Neilson's life were spent at the home of her husband's parents, Stoke Bruen, Northamptonshire. (She had married in 1864 Mr. Philip Henry Lee, the eldest son of the family.) Here she would go in the summer months, during the earlier years of her married life, and in the quiet parsonage find contentment and rest. She was, when there, constant in her attendance at the Sabbath school, and the church, and her sweet manners made her the idol of the villagers. Undoubtedly she

had a nature strongly domestic and responsive to
the endearing influences of home life. She was
also naturally a reverent person, not only in her
childhood, but throughout her life. Her mother
says she would often find her at night, kneeling beside her little cot, with her bare feet
peeping out from under her scant night-dress,
and her hands clasped before her, while her
solemn, uplifted eyes shone with a beautiful
expression as she repeated softly her simple
prayer.

The old aunt, to whose house she went the
night she left her home, had, among her treasures, a religious poem, written by Adelaide at
her request. The aunt was a devoted Methodist, and highly prized the composition, which
Adelaide's mother keeps among her treasures
now. It is mere doggerel, but is of interest, as
showing that her mind was one which could
have been easily attuned to poetic and religious
expression.

THE DYING YEAR.

At last the year has passed away,
Gone from this world of pain;
Lord, lead us in Thy path to-day,
And to begin the year again.

O Lord of beauty, God of love,
For me in blood was bathed;
The world has heard Thee from above:
Believe—and you'll be saved!

He said, O come and see,
    Ye wanderers of the earth;
He said, abide in Me:
    My love is sweet in death.

There are many incidents told of her that
show the native quality of the woman, the
richness and depth of her soul. One, in par-
ticular, which may be related here, though it
belongs to a later time:

On the occasion of one of her visits to her
mother, when they were taking an afternoon
ride together, she espied a bed of bluebells
blooming in rich profusion, and her mother
gives this account of the effect of their beauty
upon her.

She stopped the carriage, saying, "We
must stop, mother. I must go to those flowers." And when they had both reached the
place where the ground was covered with blue
blossoms, she knelt down, bent low over them
and kissed them right and left. Then she
gathered her hands full, and as she stood ar-
ranging them, looking first at them and at
those at her feet, she burst into tears, exclaim-
ing in agitated tones, "Oh! lovely, innocent
flowers: lovely, innocent flowers." Her mother
chided her kindly wishing to soothe her; but
the pain was genuine, and too deep to be con-
trolled. "Mother," she said, grasping her

parent's arm as she faced her, with the tears
streaming down her face, "Mother, I have
stood with flowers piled about me on the stage,
but never have I felt as I did kneeling here by
these blue bells—these pure, innocent flowers
that God has just fresh made." Turning
abruptly away she walked off alone, and when
she resumed her seat in the carriage she had
regained her composure, much to her mother's
relief.

Had her mother possessed the magic key
that would have unlocked the sensitive, hun-
gry nature, what rest and comfort would have
filled both hearts.

. . . .

A trip to Guiseley now, to learn of Adelaide
Neilson, would be as unsatisfactory as a visit to
Haworth to gather facts regarding Charlotte
Brontë, or her wonderful sisters. There is
simply nothing at all in the place to recall her.
She is associated with nothing there, and no
one lives who knew the real woman half so
well as did her friends in London and New
York. Her mother has been unfortunate in the
impression she has made upon the strangers who
went there after her daughter's death to learn of
her; and her refusal to confirm the statements
known to be true regarding her daughter's
early days, has led to false representations as to

her motives for keeping silence—where it would
have been well to speak—since the desire to
know the truth is a laudable one on the part
of the admirers of the great actress.

Annoyed by visitors, Mrs. Bland has removed
from the house given her by her daughter and
has gone to reside in another village. The house
in which the Blands lived for so many years has
been pulled down; so also has been the building
where Adelaide attended school. The present
home of Mrs. Bland is at Yeadon, a village a
mile distant from Guiseley. A Yorkshire
friend, who obligingly visited her recently, to
gather, if possible, some facts for this sketch,
gives me particulars of his interview in the
following letter :

I was so surprised to learn that Mrs Bland
was still in the neighborhood that I did not very
much regret the result of my profitless visit to
the schoolmaster. From there I found my way
to Swaine Hill, in Yeadon (the next village),
where I had been directed, and on asking for
the abode of Mrs. Bland was pointed to a nice,
newly-built dwelling (one of four), command-
ing a fine prospect in the direction of Guiseley,
where the old church towers might be seen
peeping over the trees and making just such a
picture as Birkett Foster loves to paint. On
trying the gate, however, I found it securely

fastened with a padlock, so was obliged to go round to the back door. A woman responded to my knock who I thought *might be* Mrs. Bland. Before I could introduce myself she at once said, "you had better go round to the front." I told her I had already tried that means of access, but had found the gate locked She motioned me to go round again, and I did so. Presently a cheerful and very polite little woman opened the gate, ushered me into the front room, asked me take a seat, and said Mrs. Bland would be with me soon. I was in a light, cheerful-looking parlor, with a bay window, the latter nicely set off with plants and the pleasant outlook I have mentioned. The room was papered with a light, showy paper. There were pictures on the walls of a cheap sort and somewhat sentimental in character. But there was one worth more than all the rest—a fine photo-portrait of Adelaide—a striking contrast to its surroundings.

In the middle of the floor was a folding (wainscot) screen covered or being covered with pictures of all sizes and colors. On the table were pictures, assorted and made ready for the screen, and a paste pot and brush.

The apartment was pretty well furnished, but it had somehow an utter absence of warmth and comfort. There were no book shelves or books to be seen.

After having been kept waiting about five minutes the door opened and in glided the person whom I had seen at the back door, and who begged me to be seated and to state the object of my visit. This was the mother of Adelaide Neilson—Mrs. Bland.

She was a fairly tall, spare woman who never could have been good looking, and who, now, was almost ugly. Not that her features were in the least misshapen or irregular—but there was something grim, cold, and severe in her face— a face that seemed never to have known a smile. Her whole appearance was sombre. In years she seemed about sixty. On her head she had something between a cap and bonnet, and everything she wore looked faded. She had the appearance of a fourth-rate tragedienne, and could not be natural however she might try. She spoke slowly and deliberately, and sometimes in so low a key as scarcely to be audible, but occasionally she would rise from her chair, stamp one foot down firmly (as if "treading the boards") and speak in a shrill, loud key. Once I felt alarmed, as I thought she could not be quite sane. But she suddenly resumed her ordinary manner, and became silent and reserved.

This description of the lady will enable you

better to understand the interview I had with
her. After having expressed (as gently and
carefully as I could) the object of my visit, she
said she was not at all surprised, for she had
had many such—in fact a great deal too many.
Newsmongers and curiosity-seekers had simply
taken her by storm since Adelaide's death. She
had had as many as twenty-seven visitors in
one day.

At first she said she was not at all reluctant
to tell what she knew about her daughter's
career, but had been so shamefully misrepre-
sented and slandered that she had quite made
up her mind never to say another word to anyone on the subject.

She then alluded to a lady who had come all
the way from America (she was really a native
of a village near Guiseley—Baildon) to pick up
all the particulars she could about Miss Neilson
and her family connections, but she had gone
about it in a strange fashion. First, she had
picked up some gossiping woman in the village,
who not only told her all she knew, but also
many things that she didn't know—pure and
complete fabrications, or in other words, bare-
faced and scandalous lies. The lady had then
returned to America and actually printed and
circulated all that she had been told by the
Guiseley woman, without having taken the

trouble to ascertain whether there was any truth in what she stated. This "American lady" I take it was the one who wrote the narrative you sent me to read. Mrs. Bland is terribly incensed against her. She said she had been strongly advised to bring an action against her for libel.

Interrupting her as rarely as I could, I tried to draw her into a general conversation about Adelaide, but with indifferent success. "No," she said, "you must not ask a single question about my daughter, for I shall not answer it. I am not treating you with any more disrespect than I treat others, but I have made a vow and heaven helping me I will keep it!" (Here she began to be tragic.) "I have been shamefully and outrageously betrayed," she exclaimed, "but my poor, dead child will some day be avenged, as sure as there is a God above!" "I am but a woman, but there is a spirit within me that people know not of. My slanderous enemies I could persecute to the death!" I tried to appease and soothe her as much as possible, and she gradually became calmer.

If her "enemies" were good at making false statements, she was equally good at denying them. In fact she denied everything. Adelaide (she said) had never worked in a factory; had never been a nurse-girl, either for Mrs. Padgett

or anybody else; had never run away from home
—in short, she had never done anything at all
that people said she had. Mrs. Bland wanted
to give me the impression that as her daughter
became a great actress, she was born great,
and that everything about her was great. This
greatness she seems determined to uphold, but,
alas, the family is too well known at Guiseley.
Adelaide was a dutiful child and her filial regard
took the practical shape of leaving her mother
in good circumstances. Mrs. Bland seems now
very anxious to forget the days of poverty,
when Lizzie was a poor girl running about the
fields and lanes of Guiseley, and she is annoyed that this period in the family history
should now be spoken of. It is absurd for
her to cherish such views. In an interview
I had with Mr. Shuttleworth, the organist at
Guiseley Church at the time when Miss Neilson
visited it, that gentleman, long a resident in
Guiseley, told me that Mrs. Bland was alto-
gether wrong in denying the statements that
her daughter had worked in a factory, been a
nurse-girl, and run away. He was very much
surprised at her attempt to repudiate such
plain facts.

Mrs. Bland professed great affection for her
talented daughter. She said she had taken
Adelaide's death so much to heart, that for

several weeks she could eat nothing. At last the doctor told her that if she did not cease such fretting she could not live long.

She remembered her son, a young man, her only remaining offspring, and thought it best not to die at present. I must confess to being out of all patience with her maudlin and sentimental way of expressing her sympathetic feelings. " Poor, dear Adelaide," she exclaimed, "she was indeed an angel upon earth." Going to a small cupboard she brought out a scrapbook or album, which she placed on the table for me to look at. Turning over the leaves I saw a wonderful collection of (dried) flowers which she said had been sent her (Mrs. Bland) from nearly all parts of the world. " This," she said, pointing to one. " was given to me by my friend Lord " (somebody, I don't recollect who), " and *that* (pointing to another) I received from Count——." On one page were some written verses signed at the foot " A. Bland." "These lines." she said, " I wrote shortly after my daughter's death." She begged me to read them. I did so and found them to be sheer nonsense. I did not say so, but instead made some remark expressive of surprise that to her other qualifications she added that of poet. "Oh, yes!" she exclaimed, " the power of expressing my thoughts in verse has

been a great comfort to me. It is surprising
how we poets do live in a world of our own.
Ordinary, common-place people cannot understand us." I merely said, "indeed," and, more
for the sake of saying something, than for any
better reason, I asked if she would kindly al-
low me to take a copy of the verses. She, however, declined. The book contained several
other effusions of hers, which I did not read.
The flowers were, indeed, very fine, and I fancy
the book had been Adelaide's.

I did not, of course, venture to say a word
concerning Miss Neilson's father. Had I done
so the consequences might have been serious
to me. He is a mystery and likely to remain so.

As I found it impossible to gain anything
from Mrs. Bland, I wished her good-bye, and
thanked her for the interview she had allowed
me. She saw me to the door very graciously,
and I left her, disappointed at my inability to
learn more of her wonderfully-gifted daughter.

While in the village I made inquiries of both
Mr. Frizell and Mr. Shuttleworth as to places
of interest associated with the name of Lizzie
Bland that I might sketch, but found there was
absolutely nothing. The house in which Lizzie
and her mother lived had been pulled down: so
had the school-house to which Lizzie had gone.
I made a sketch of the house in which Mrs.

Bland now lives, which I enclose. There is nothing more to be learnt of the famous actress in that quarter.

.   .   .   .

Of Miss Neilson's life as an actress it is not possible in this sketch to make more than mention. After a career of unvarying success in Great Britain, she came to this country in 1872, and made her first appearance at Booth's Theatre as *Juliet*. Her tour from city to city was a triumphal march, and she left the United States richer in reputation and money. In the autumn of 1874 she returned, and was as warmly received. This time she made her debut at Booth's Theatre as *Amy Robsart*, and appeared as *Julia*, in "The Hunchback," as *Pauline* in "The Lady of Lyons," and as *Juliet*. Her success was complete in every *role* she assumed, and she was the dramatic idol of the day.

Again she came and her success was marked. When on the night of May 8th she bade adieu to her New York friends, Mr. William Winter wrote, in the *Tribune*, this farewell:

"Since the night when Dickens, with slow step and sad face, made his last exit from the stage of Steinway Hall, there has been no theatrical sensation in this city at once so animated with chivalry and so touching with sense of sorrow and loss. We shall see other actresses whose powers are as distinct, who are unique in one element or another, and potent on some one line of art; we are not likely again to see an actress in whom are combined as they have revealed themselves in her the attributes of power, fire, tenderness and grace. She is exceptional in this, and that is the reason her career has been one of conquest and continued popularity."

On her first two visits to America Adelaide Neilson was accompanied by her husband, Philip Lee. Their domestic relations which for some years were happy, became otherwise, and in 1877 they were divorced, the decree being obtained by her in the Supreme Court, New York. That season, '76–77, she gave one hundred performances in the United States, under the management of Mr. Strakosch.

She had been married fourteen years when she was divorced, and the incident, and the circumstances coupled with it, affected her greatly. In the early years of her married life she was deeply attached to her husband, and to his family. After her divorce she frequently expressed a determination to retire from the stage, and at the close of her season here in 1879 her theatrical wardrobe was sold, and she left this country intending to have some years of private life. Lovers of Shakespeare the world over regretted to hear of this step, because she was the embodiment of his characters, and there was none to interpret them as she did. For centuries men had read of *Juliet* and *Rosalind*, *Beatrice* and *Viola*, but in imagination only had they pictured them. Neilson came and she was each and all. She was "Shakespeare's woman," brilliant and captivating in all her artistic and personal characteristics—alone in these—while she was the peer of all who had preceded her in the representations she made her own.

A critic writing of her performance at a Shakespearean Reading which she gave in New York in 1874, says of her:

' In Miss Neilson are combined the tenderest feminine loveliness with that intelligence which apprehends all meanings through the heart, and as long as man's mind is robust and wholesome such a union of attributes will have a power in the mental world. . . . No man who heard her read the "May Queen," in the pathetic part of which the tears rained from her eyes, will forget it to the last day of the longest life. To hear words of such glee and such solemn tenderness from lips so lovely and a heart so fond of good is to know what poetry means—in that interior essence which, to use Moore's fine figure, is the fragrance of the wood that grows precious as it burns. In other parts she was sweet and grave, like some angelic child. She manifested a fine talent in the lighter comedy, a great deal of true humor, and a fire of martial enthusiasm. Certain vocal exploits, such as the crier's speech in the Ingoldsby Legend, showed her resources of voice and evoked delighted plaudits. The rarer merit was the deeper one of emotion always adequate, taste always true, if we except one bit in the selection from Congreve, and refinement pervading and adorning all."

The portraits accompanying this sketch represent her in the famous characters she essayed,

and her beautiful personality is recalled in each
and all. In studying them one may well ex-
claim in Shakespeare's words:

"She hath a holy gift of prophecy,
And sundry blessings hung about her head
That showed her full of grace."

Some one has described fascination to be "the
magnetism of imagination and thought," and
the definition is applicable to the character of
Miss Neilson; she had the magnetism of a sin-
cere and trusting nature; hers was a kind and
unselfish soul, and her very faults were the mis-
directed growths of her finest qualities. Her
impetuosity was offset by a docile, forgiving
spirit, and as child and woman she was sensitive to kindness and appreciative of recogni-
tion. Of all who knew her in her Yorkshire
home, not one but emphasizes her gentle be-
havior, her native refinement. Viewed from the
loftiest altitude of mind everything that comes
to a life is recognized as the best thing for its
permanent welfare, even if through the world's
conventional lens it seems otherwise. Whatever
may have been the shortcomings of her life,
however much she may have wronged herself,
it is well to believe, with the Buddhists, that
we are born into this world to rid ourselves of
certain inherent weaknesses and failings, and
that we get rid of them in suffering the conse-

quences they bring to us. Through discipline
and pain her soul fitted itself for the higher
conditions of the life she now knows.

Her voice, than which there is no surer in-
dication of character in man or woman, was
soft and sweet as a child's, and had a cadence
in her maturer years which touched the ear of
all who heard it ; it was appealing, pathetic,
melodious. Her mouth was more beautiful
in expression than in outline ; and this is
true of all her features, with the exception of her
eyes, which were large and lustrous. Her head
was small and shapely, and her ruddy brown
hair well suited the pale, olive-tinted complex-
ion. She was slight of form and queenly in
bearing.

Her's was a personality pre-eminently
adapted for the Shakespearean juvenile characters she assumed so unapproachably ; and
could the great dramatist, looking back over
the centuries of time, have seen the visible em-
bodiments of the characters he drew in *Rosalind, Viola, Beatrice, Juliet,* we cannot doubt
that he would have been enraptured with
the spectacle. As *Juliet* she was most admired,
and it is with this character that her name is
and will continue to be associated. Nothing
could have been more beautiful than her per-
sonation of the Veronese maiden. She was

an entrancingly lovely picture as she danced with stately step the ancient *minuet;* or stood leaning over the moonlit balcony of her father's house with her ardent lover below.

At Boston among her audience one night was the venerable poet Longfellow, who wrote her the next day : "I thank you for your beautiful interpretation of this enchanting character. I have never in my life seen intellectual and poetical feeling more exquisitely combined." He sent her some verses which her acting had inspired, which he asked her to keep unpublished. They are said to be now in the possession of her mother.

It is related that on one occasion while in Richmond, Virginia, she went to the capitol where the Legislature was in session. Some of the members perceiving her in the ladies' gallery, business was immediately at a standstill. She soon had half the members about her, and was compelled to retire from their presence in order that business might proceed.

She was undoubtedly the most gifted actress of her time, and perhaps the most fascinating of any time. Her audiences were literally in love with her; there was a charm about her that was irresistible.

She has been said to resemble Nell Gwynn, not in her professional characteristics, but in personal qualities. Like that celebrated actress, she was generous to a fault, and, like her, she suffered through the exercise of this noble trait in many ways. Both these women were illegitimate, and both were the most popular English actresses of their day. Here the likeness is at an end, for Neilson was superior to all others in the magnetic genius she possessed, and was so truly beautiful that to have seen her is to have a memory too pleasing ever to be forgotten. Mr. William Winter, of the New York *Tribune*, who, as well as Mr. Joseph Knight, of the London *Athenæum*, was one of her kindest and most appreciative critics, said of her after her first performance of *Juliet* in this country:

"An able copy of a lovely ideal, and whether true or false, a charmingly sweet embodiment."

"Miss Neilson's *Juliet*," the critic continues, "is a young, beautiful, passionate, Italian girl, impetuous in all things, proud, but gentle, fiery, but tender, capricious, but true—to whom mere existence is an ardent joy, and to whom first love comes like a revelation from heaven. *Juliet* is not a part that requires a great actress, but it requires a very good one, and it had on this occasion one of the best that have come to these shores. Miss Neilson's personelle has not been exaggerated by her portraits. She is slender in figure, but not attenuated; her head is small; her features are regular; her eyes are dark and luminous; her hair is brown; her mouth is full and sensitive; her voice is very sweet; and the carriage of her head and person denotes a bright intelligence and pure refinement that are very gratifying to the sense of entire beauty which invites moral, mental and physical clearness and worth."

During her last engagement here, which ended in May, 1880, she was supported by Mr. Edward Compton, an artist of fine ability, who came over with her from England. He was a son of Henry Compton, a famous comedian of the old English school. His mother, who was an actress of ability, was a daughter of Henry Montague, a brilliant light comedian in the early part of the century. It was not known to many, but a few of her closest friends in America were aware that Mr. Compton and Miss Neilson were married, and that her retirement from the stage was to be followed, so soon as she returned to England, by an announcement of the marriage and a quiet home life for some time to come. Miss Neilson's long winter's work had told upon her strength; she was weary and tired when she returned to New York from San Francisco, to take her departure for Europe. The voyage did her little good,

yet she hoped to rest on the Continent a little
while before returning to England to reside
permanently. She was in Paris with her husband and traveling companion on the 14th of
August, and on the 15th took a ride in the Bois
de Boulogne. Feeling faint from the heat, she
asked for a glass of iced milk and drank it
with a grateful sense of relief. Shortly afterward she was seized with neuralgic cramps in
the stomach, a disease from which she had long
suffered at intervals. Mr. Compton hastened
with her to the Chalet Restaurant and she was
removed from the carriage and placed on a sofa
in the reception room. There she died after
twelve hours of intense agony. There was no
hope from the first, as was shown by the *post
mortem* examination, for her illness was a com-
plication of troubles, and death was the only
possible end.

The shocking news of her sudden death sad-
dened the people of two countries, and particulars of the event were eagerly sought for by
loving hearts the world over. Some of the sad
facts were never given. Mr. Compton, power-
less to resist French law, saw her body hastened away to the public morgue, there to be
subjected to a *post mortem* examination, and
friendless and alone, he and Mrs. Goodall waited
until the body was finally given to their charge.

One other mourner joined them at the morgue,
a white-haired, elderly man, whose grief touched
even the officials who saw him bend over the
body of the woman he had loved so long and
steadfastly. This old friend was Admiral Glyn,
to whom in a sudden impulse of generosity,
before she had thought of marrying again, she
willed the larger portion of her property. Thus,
though she died so suddenly and in a foreign
land, she had three friends with her, one of
whom was her husband.

They carried her body to England, and one
bright, sunny morning, when the birds were
singing in every tree and hedge-row, they laid
it away at Brompton, in the presence of many
friends who had followed it to its resting-place.
Over the grave had been spread a covering of
royal purple velvet, and in this cloth of kings
they laid the flower-laden oaken coffin; wreaths
of lilies were placed upon it and the dead *Juliet*
was enshrined in blossoms. Then, as the
casket was slowly lowered to its last resting
place, those who stood about the open grave
drew nigh with their offerings, and in a few
moments the lovely woman was buried, not in
cold earth, but in a bed of flowers whose per-
fume filled the air.

Over her grave was reared the tall cross, re-
produced in this Souvenir, with its fitting and

touching inscriptions. And there, in that old London cemetery, sleeps "Shakespeare's woman," the first and the last of her kind.

Dead, when love and home long dreamed of were hers ; when the sweet anticipations of domestic life were just awakening in her heart feelings too sacred to be shared with the world.

What a fate was hers ! What a triumph and yet what a mockery was her life !—her own tragedy the saddest of any she had ever personated—her death crueler than any she had ever depicted !

With her sweet voice hushed forever, one at her grave might well have exclaimed, with Edna Dean Proctor,

"Lord ! doth thou see how dread a thing is death,
  When silence such as this is all it leaves,
 To watch in agony the parting breath,
   Till the fond eyes are closed, the dear voice still,
 And know that not the wildest prayer can thrill
   Thee to awake her; but our grief must fill
 Alike the rosy morns, the rainy eves."

Said her kind friend, Mr. Winter, when news of her loss had reached us here : " Whatever may have been the vicissitudes, trials, mistakes and sorrows of her past, she was by nature a woman of pure, domestic tastes—affectionate, gentle, confiding and true, and she would have made that home very happy with the husband whom she had chosen. . . . .

IN LOVING MEMORY OF
ADELAIDE NEILSON.
DIED AUGUST 15TH 1880.

GIFTED AND BEAUTIFUL
— RESTING —

She was, to have done so much, a very young
woman. She was, in this sense, a prodigy—and
whatever were her faults and errors, it is remarkable that she bore so well the always per-
ilous burdens of early triumph, and the in-
cense of a world's admiration. She had the
intuitions of genius, and also its quick spirit
and wild temperament. She was largely ruled
by her imaginations and her feelings, and had
neither the prudence of selfishness nor the craft
of experience. Such a nature might easily go
to shipwreck and ruin. She outrode all the
storms of a passionate, wayward youth, and
anchored safe at last in the haven of duty. Her
image as it rises in memory now, is not that of
the actress who stormed the citadel of all hearts
in the delirium of *Juliet*, or dazzled with the
witchery of *Rosalind's* glee or *Viola's* tender
grace, but it is of the grave, sweet woman,
who playing softly in the twilight, sang in that
rich, tremulous, touching voice, an anthem that
paraphrases the words of Christ : 'With all
your sorrows I am made partaker, and am ac-
quainted with all your griefs.'"

And then he wrote these last words—words
tenderly cherished by all who loved her :

"And O, to think the sun can shine,
The birds can sing, the flowers can bloom,
And she, whose soul was all divine,
Be darkly mouldering in the tomb;

That o'er her head the night-wind sighs,
   And the sad cypress droops and mourns;
That night has veiled her glorious eyes,
   And silence hushed her heavenly tones.

That those sweet lips no more can smile,
   Nor pity's tender shadows chase,
With many a gentle, child-like wile,
   The rippling laughter o'er her face:

That dust is on the burnished gold
   That floated round her royal head;
That her great heart is dead and cold—
   Her form of fire and beauty dead!

Roll on, gray earth and shining star,
   And coldly mock our dreams of bliss;
There is no glory left to mar,
   Nor any grief so black as this!"

Adelaide Neilson died in the fullness of her prime, and for her doubtless it was best. For those who loved her, she "sleeps too early and too long." We hold her in tender memory and have hesitated so long to say good-bye, that we will omit it now, and in some brighter clime bid her " good morning !"

www.ingramcontent.com/pod-product-compliance
Lightning Source LLC
Chambersburg PA
CBHW030009030726
47499CB00008B/2971